Dear Parents:

Congratulations! Your child is tak
the first steps on an exciting journey.
The destination? Independent reading!

STEP INTO READING® will help your child get there. The program offers
five steps to reading success. Each step includes fun stories and colorful
art or photographs. In addition to original fiction and books with favorite
characters, there are Step into Reading Non-Fiction Readers, Phonics Readers
and Boxed Sets, Sticker Readers, and Comic Readers—a complete literacy
program with something to interest every child.

Learning to Read, Step by Step!

Ready to Read   Preschool–Kindergarten
• big type and easy words • rhyme and rhythm • picture clues
For children who know the alphabet and are eager to
begin reading.

Reading with Help   Preschool–Grade 1
• basic vocabulary • short sentences • simple stories
For children who recognize familiar words and sound out
new words with help.

Reading on Your Own   Grades 1–3
• engaging characters • easy-to-follow plots • popular topics
For children who are ready to read on their own.

Reading Paragraphs   Grades 2–3
• challenging vocabulary • short paragraphs • exciting stories
For newly independent readers who read simple sentences
with confidence.

Ready for Chapters   Grades 2–4
• chapters • longer paragraphs • full-color art
For children who want to take the plunge into chapter books
but still like colorful pictures.

STEP INTO READING® is designed to give every child a successful
reading experience. The grade levels are only guides; children will progress
through the steps at their own speed, developing confidence in their reading.
The F&P Text Level on the back cover serves as another tool to help you
choose the right book for your child.

Remember, a lifetime love of reading starts with a single step!

For my sons, Jessie and Christopher. I taught you how to read, and you taught me how to love unconditionally. My hope is that you always dance to the beat of your own drum. —A.S.

Visit us on the Web!
StepIntoReading.com
rhcbooks.com

Educators and librarians, for a variety of teaching tools, visit us at RHTeachersLibrarians.com

Library of Congress Cataloging-in-Publication Data
Names: Showers, April, author. | Conley, Anthony, illustrator.
Title: A magical parade / by April Showers ; illustrated by Anthony Conley.
Description: First edition. | New York : Random House, 2024. | Series: Afro Unicorn |
Audience: Ages 4–6. | Summary: The Afro Unicorns, Divine, Magical, and Unique, work together to have the best parade and Day of Crowns ever.
Identifiers: LCCN 2023036078 (print) | LCCN 2023036079 (ebook) | ISBN 978-0-593-70415-8 (pbk.) | ISBN 978-0-593-80696-8 (lib. bdg.) | ISBN 978-0-593-70416-5 (ebook)
Subjects: LCSH: Unicorns—Fiction. | Parades—Fiction. | LCGFT: Picture books.
Classification: LCC PZ7.1.S51786 Map 2024 (print) | LCC PZ7.1.S51786 (ebook) | DDC [E]—dc23

Printed in the United States of America
10 9 8 7 6 5 4 3 2 1
First Edition

This book has been officially leveled by using the F&P Text Level Gradient™ Leveling System.

A Magical Parade

Afro Unicorn®

by April Showers

illustrated by Anthony Conley

Random House 🏠 New York

Wake up,
Afro Unicorns!
It is the big day!

Today is the
Day of Crowns.

It only happens
once a year!

The Afro Unicorns are getting ready.

Unique sings in
the rainbow shower.

Divine dips her
hooves in glitter.

Magical picks out
ribbons for her mane.

It is time for
the best part.

It is time to put on their special crowns!

When they wear
the special crowns,
the Afro Unicorns
feel like they can
do anything!

They are strong.

They are kind.

They are Afro Unicorns!

The Afro Unicorns
walk into town.
There are so many
colors!

There are so many
Afro Unicorns!
Every Afro Unicorn
wears a crown.

A unicorn comes up
to the friends.

The unicorn
looks upset.

The unicorn has lost
their crown!

The unicorn was
going to lead
the parade.
Now the unicorn
is too scared
to lead.

The friends know
what to do.

Magical and Divine
ask if the unicorn
wants a hug.

A hug is nice!

Unique has an idea.

She tells the other
Afro Unicorns
her idea.

The Afro Unicorns
pick flowers.
They find sparkly
things.

They make a
new crown!

The unicorn loves
the new crown.

The unicorn asks their
new friends to lead
the parade with them!

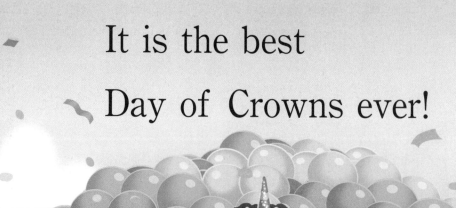

It is the best
Day of Crowns ever!